BUDDY'S
BEDTIME BATTERY

To Willie, Lucie, and George,
the lights of my life.
"I'll see you in the morning, like I always do."
—C.G.

To my grandson Grady
—T.B.

 Published in the United States by Random House Children's Books,
a division of Penguin Random House LLC, New York.

Random House and the colophon are registered trademarks of Penguin Random House LLC.

Visit us on the Web! randomhousekids.com

Educators and librarians, for a variety of teaching tools, visit us at RHTeachersLibrarians.com

Library of Congress Cataloging-in-Publication Data is available upon request.
ISBN 978-0-553-51339-4 (trade) — ISBN 978-0-375-97468-7 (lib. bdg.) — ISBN 978-0-553-51340-0 (ebook)

Printed in the United States of America
10 9 8 7 6 5 4 3 2
First Edition

Random House Children's Books supports
the First Amendment and celebrates the right to read.

BUDDY'S BEDTIME BATTERY

by Christina Geist

illustrated by

Tim Bowers

Random House New York

"I am *not* a boy!" yells Buddy, looking in the mirror at his new jammies.

"I am a robot! I am Ro-Buddy!"

“BEEP! My battery is on!
I can walk and talk!”

“Alert, Ro-Buddy,” says Robo-Mom in a voice that sounds like the movies. “Please turn on your jumping button and get your energy out!”

Ro-Buddy jumps on his mini trampoline until his turbo charger is . . .

. . . BEEP! . . . worn out.

"Okay, Ro-Buddy! Visit the space station potty and get ready to power down."

Ro-Buddy makes a laser-beam pee-pee. He cleans his metallic hands with super-sensitive germ-blaster wipes.

His human sister, Lady, helps Ro-Buddy brush his teeth so he doesn't get water all over his electric body parts.

Ro-Buddy switches on his gentle button.

He climbs into the reading chair and lets Robo-Mom run her hands through his crazy robot hair.

He listens with his supersonic ears as she reads three books. He looks at the pictures until his super-duper eyeballs start to feel . . . BEEP! . . . low on battery.

“Time to activate your cuddle pod,” says Robo-Dad. “Take a deep breath before we power down your battery.”

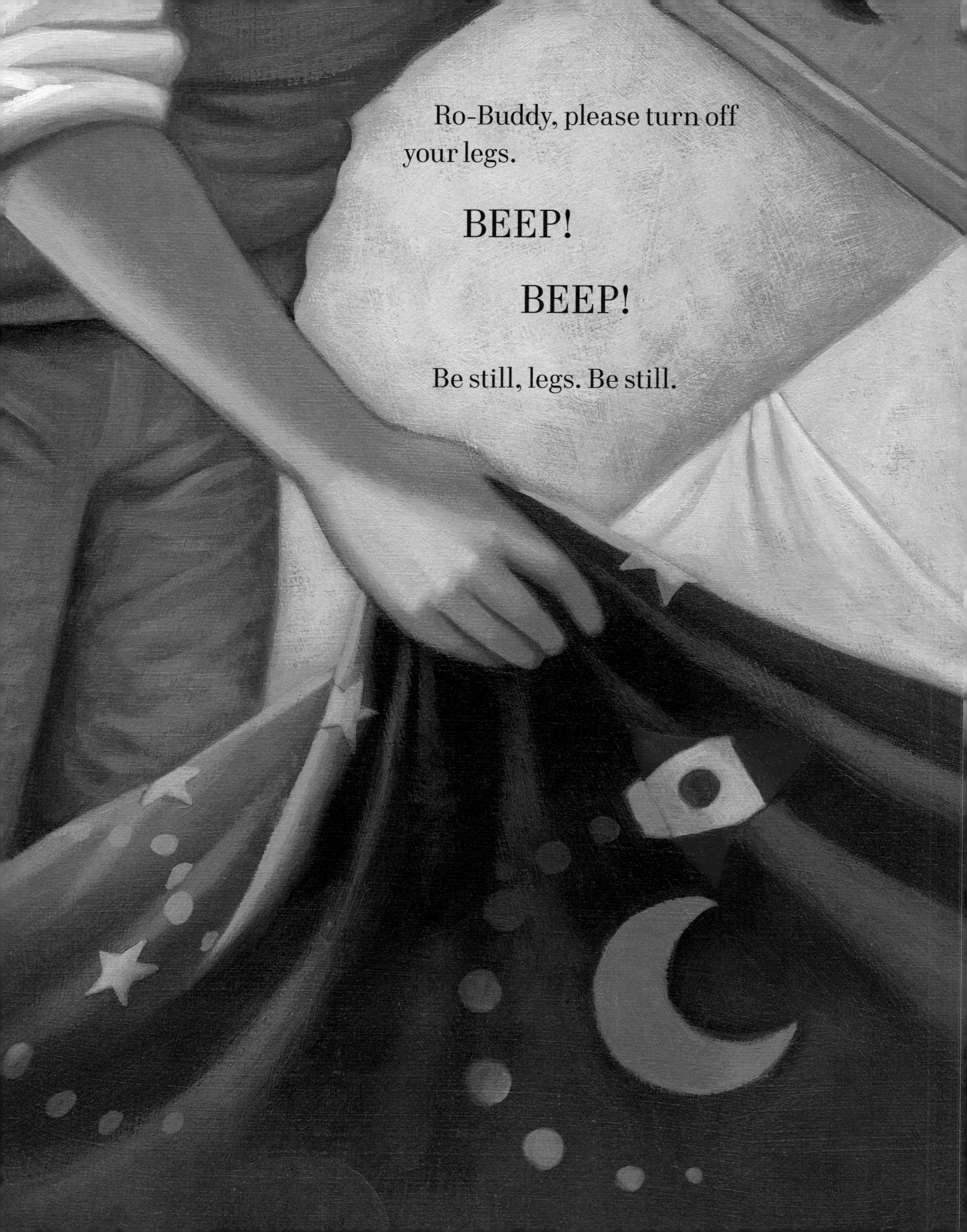

Ro-Buddy, please turn off your legs.

BEEP!

BEEP!

Be still, legs. Be still.

Ro-Buddy, shake your tush and shut it down.

SHAKE.

SHAKE.

BEEP!

Be still, tushy.
Be still.

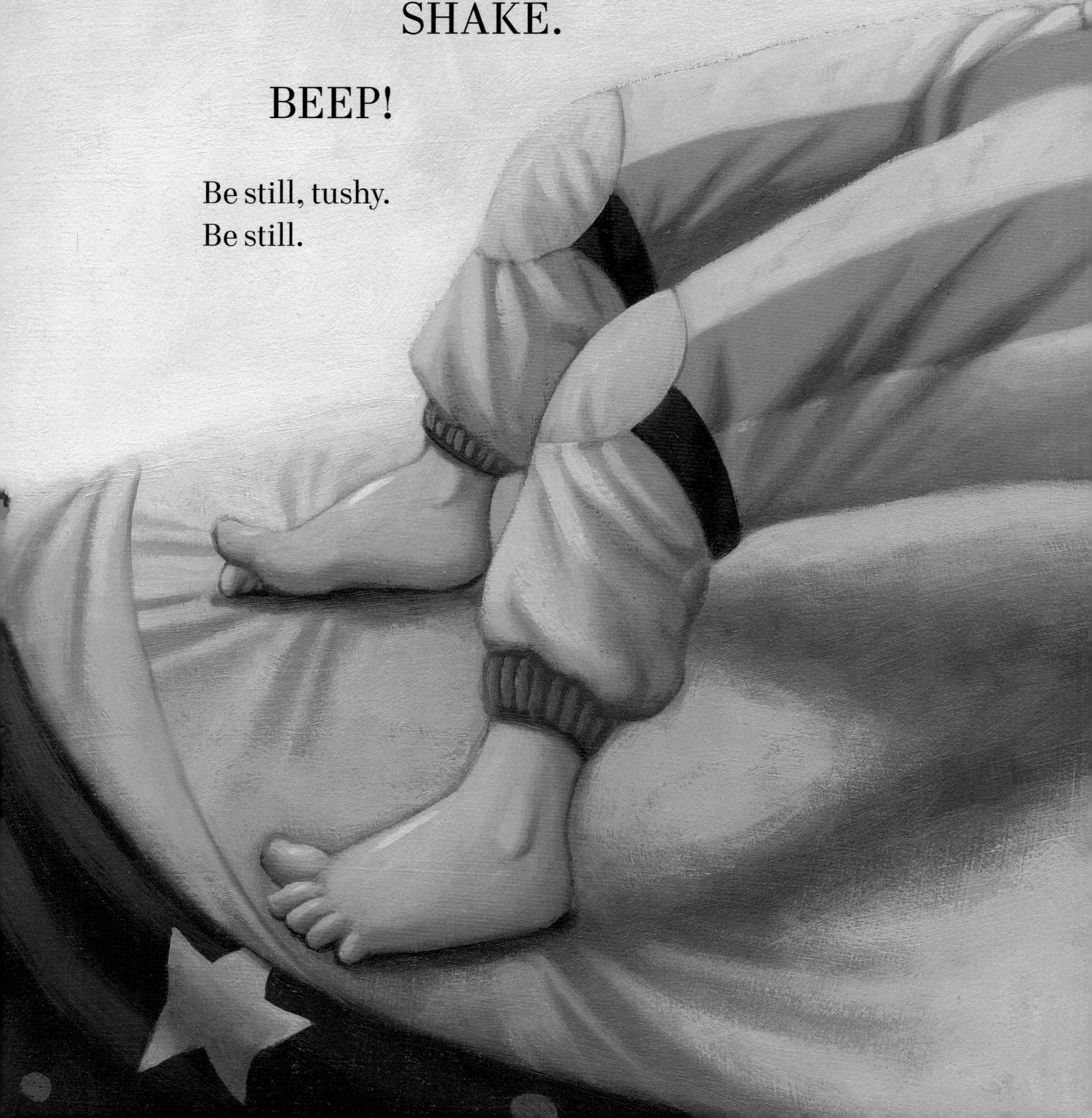

And power down your belly button.

SQUISH.

BEEP!

Be still, belly.
Be still.

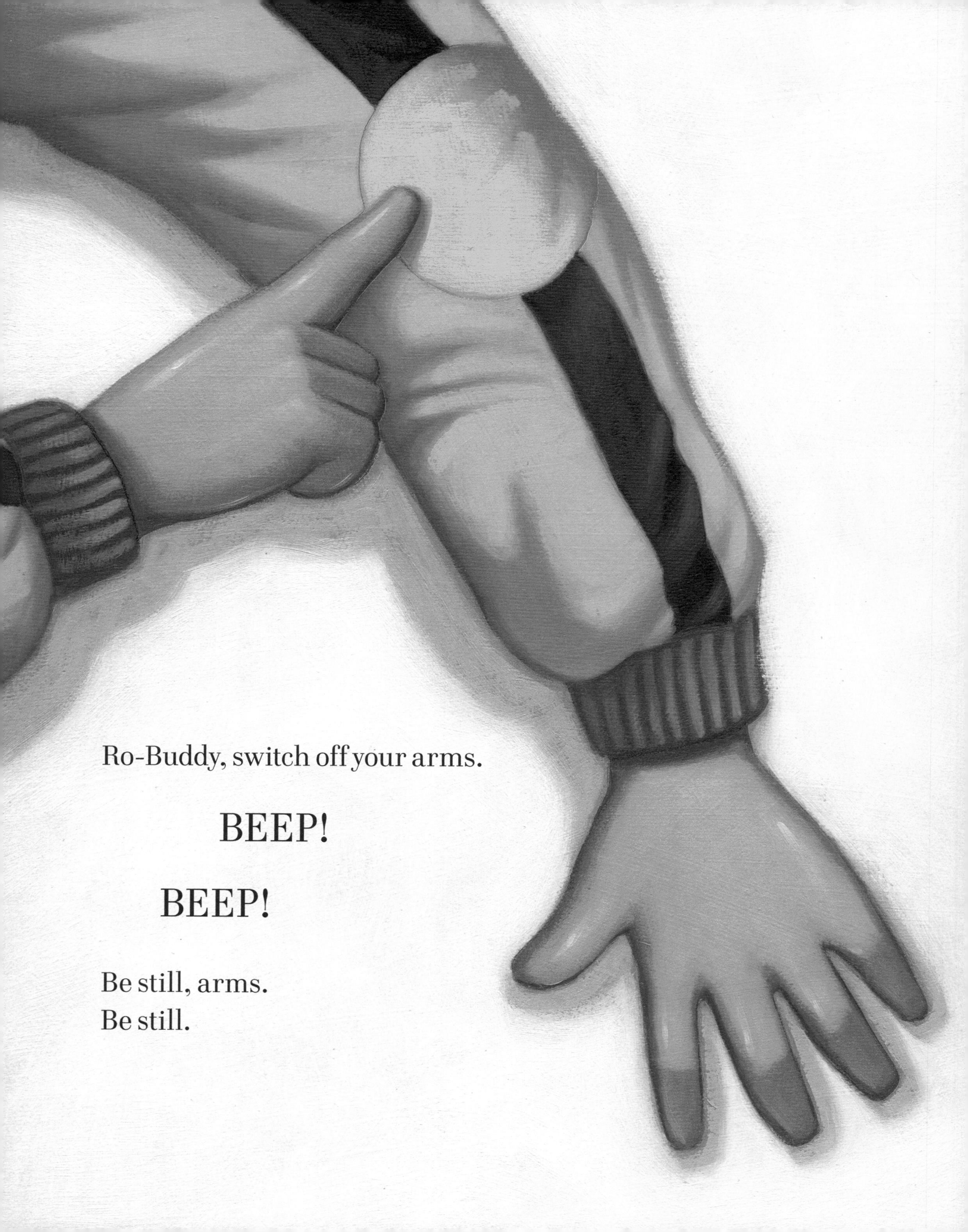

Ro-Buddy, switch off your arms.

BEEP!

BEEP!

Be still, arms.
Be still.

And power down your face.

Eyes.

BEEP!

Nose.

BEEP!

Ears.

BEEP!

Mouth.

BEEP!

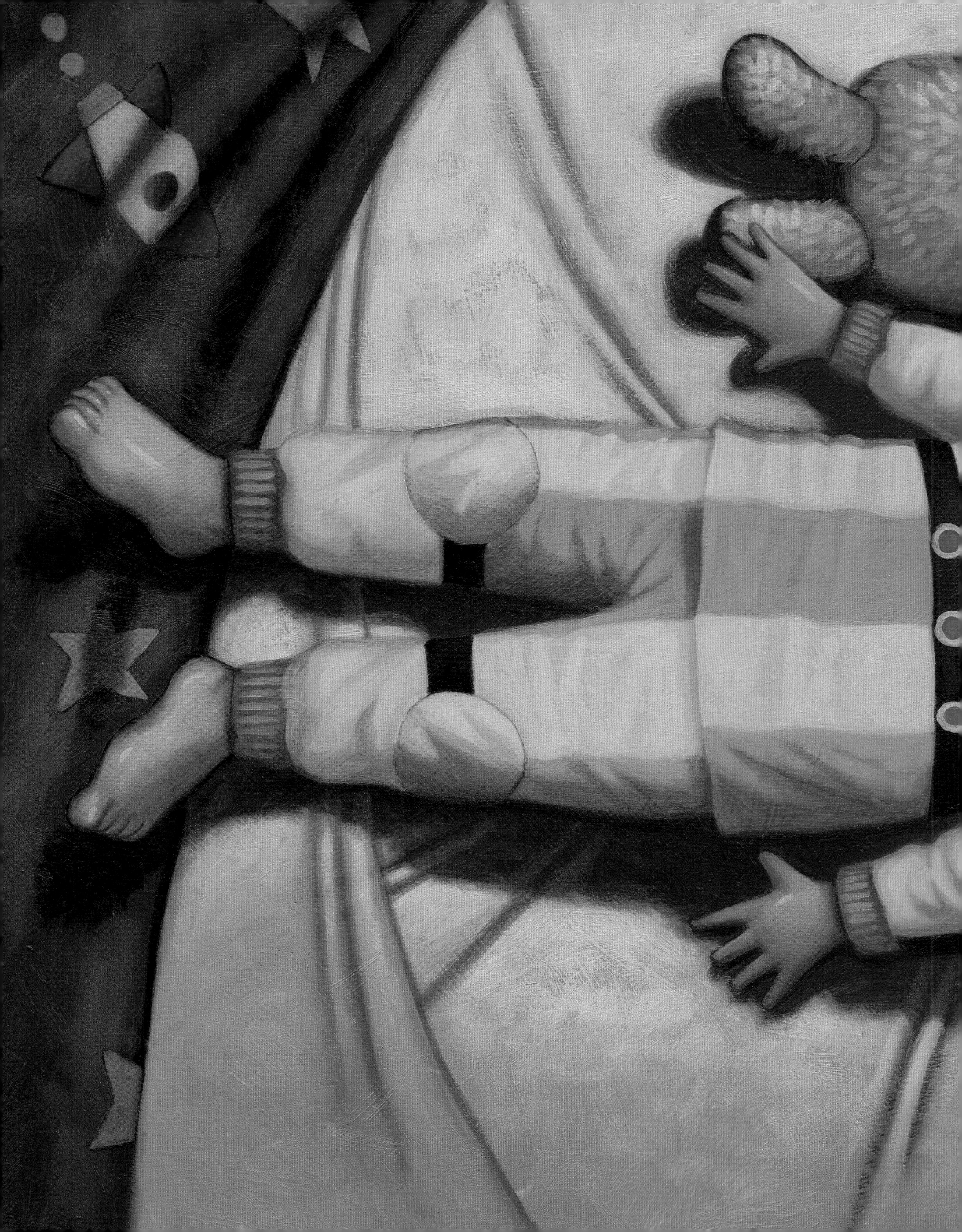

Be still, face.
Be still.

Last one, Ro-Buddy. Please squeeze your snuggle puppy and then turn off your hands.

WOOF! WOOF!

BEEP! BEEP!

Be still, hands.
Be still.

Robo-Mom and Robo-Dad push Ro-Buddy's big red power button very, very softly.

Beep.

Be still, Ro-Buddy.

Be still.

Shhh. Good night.

ALERT!

ALERT!

Ro-Buddy is out of his cuddle pod! He's walking around in the middle of the night!

Back to your pod, Ro-Buddy. Shhh. Here's a little sip of water. Oh, no. Your puppy was on the floor. Here he is.

There now . . . power down again . . . back to sleep.

Shhhhhhhhh.

Beeeeeeeeeeeeeep.